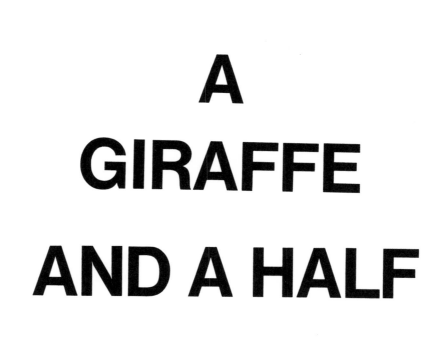

A
GIRAFFE
AND A HALF

by Shel Silverstein

HARPER & ROW, PUBLISHERS

If you had a giraffe...

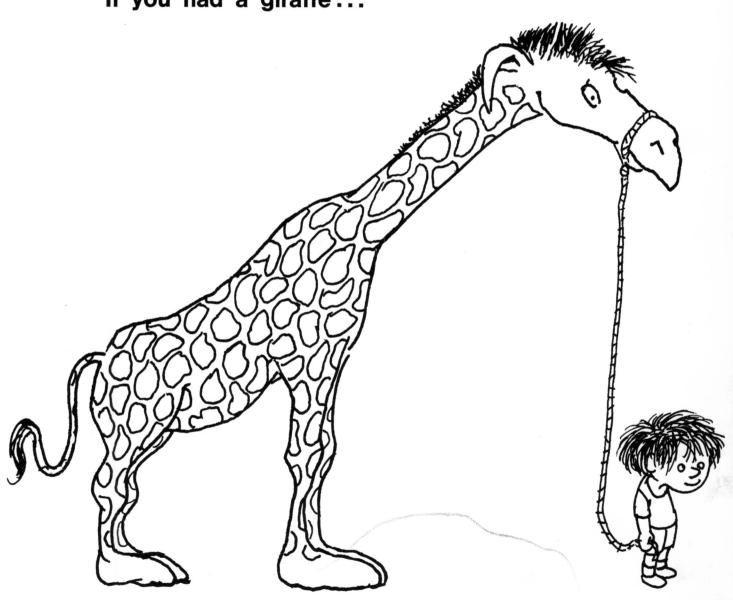

and he stretched

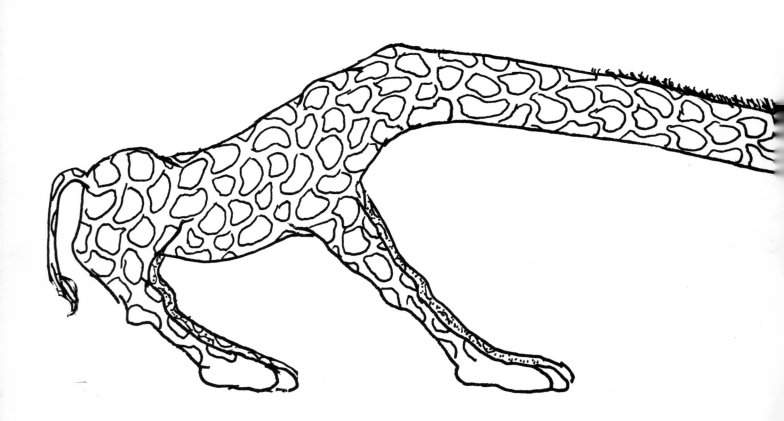

another half...

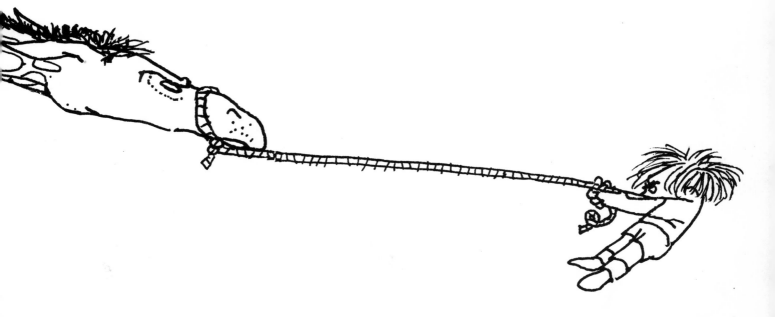

you would have

a giraffe and a half.

If he put on a hat
and inside lived a rat...

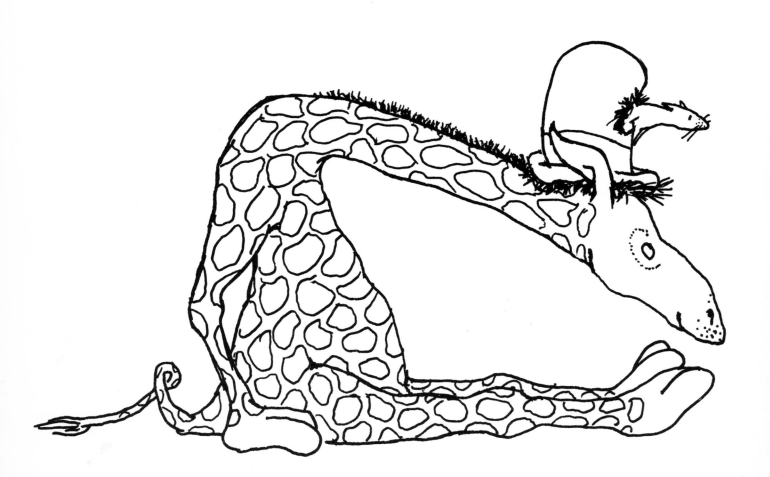

you would have a giraffe and a half
with a rat in his hat.

If you dressed him in a suit
and he looked very cute . . .

you would have a giraffe and a half
with a rat in his hat
looking cute in a suit.

If you glued a rose
to the tip of his nose...

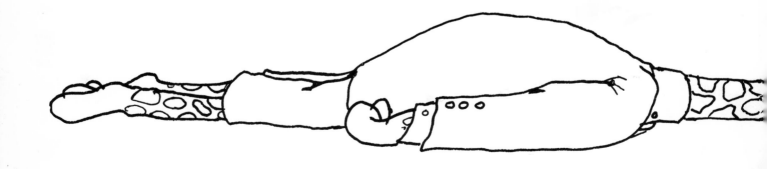

you would have a giraffe and a half
with a rat in his hat
looking cute in a suit
with a rose on his nose.

If a bumbley old bee
stung him right on the knee...

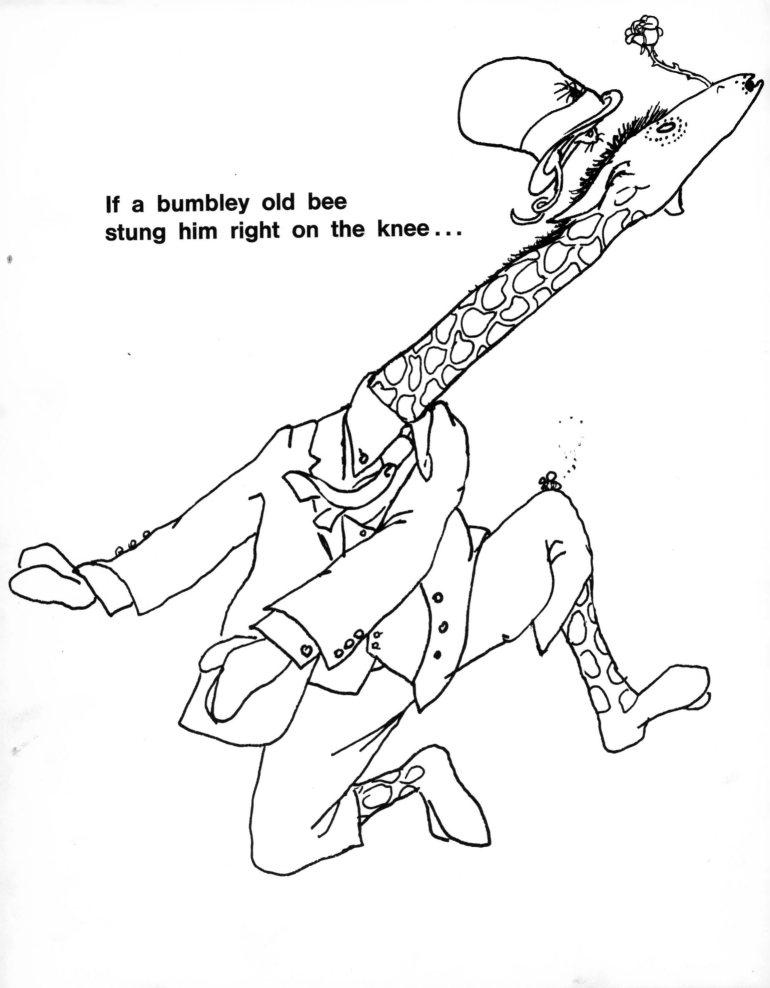

you would have a giraffe and a half
with a rat in his hat
looking cute in a suit
with a rose on his nose
and a bee on his knee.

If he put on a shoe
and then stepped in some glue...

you would have a giraffe and a half
with a rat in his hat
looking cute in a suit
with a rose on his nose
and a bee on his knee
and some glue on his shoe.

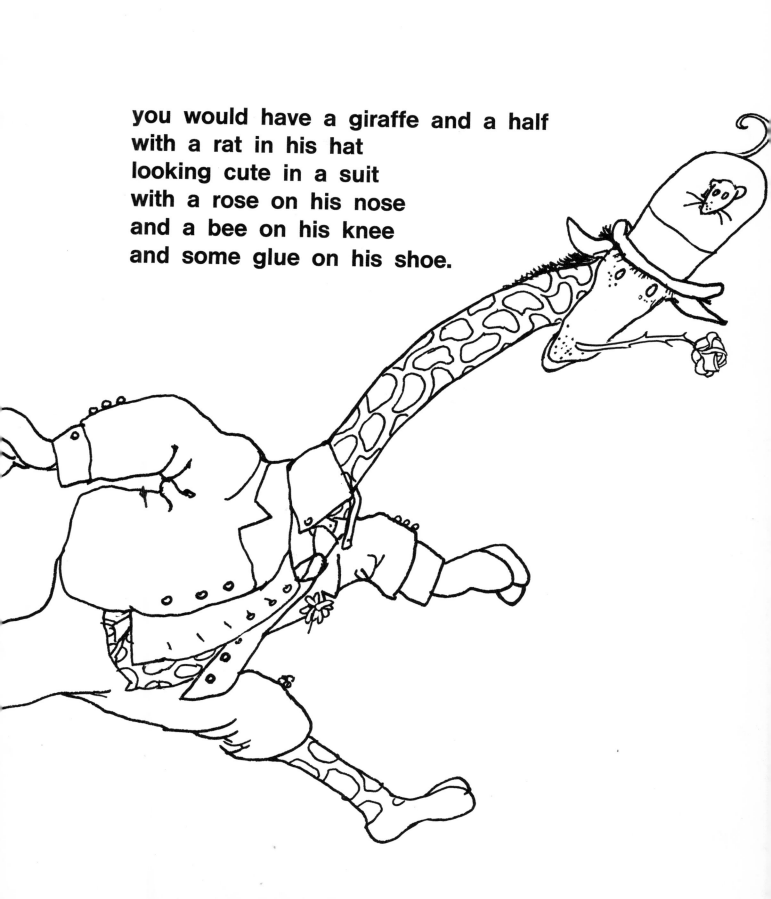

If you gave him a flute
and he played tooty-toot...

you would have a giraffe and a half
with a rat in his hat
looking cute in a suit
with a rose on his nose
and a bee on his knee
and some glue on his shoe
playing toot on a flute.

If he used a chair
to comb his hair...

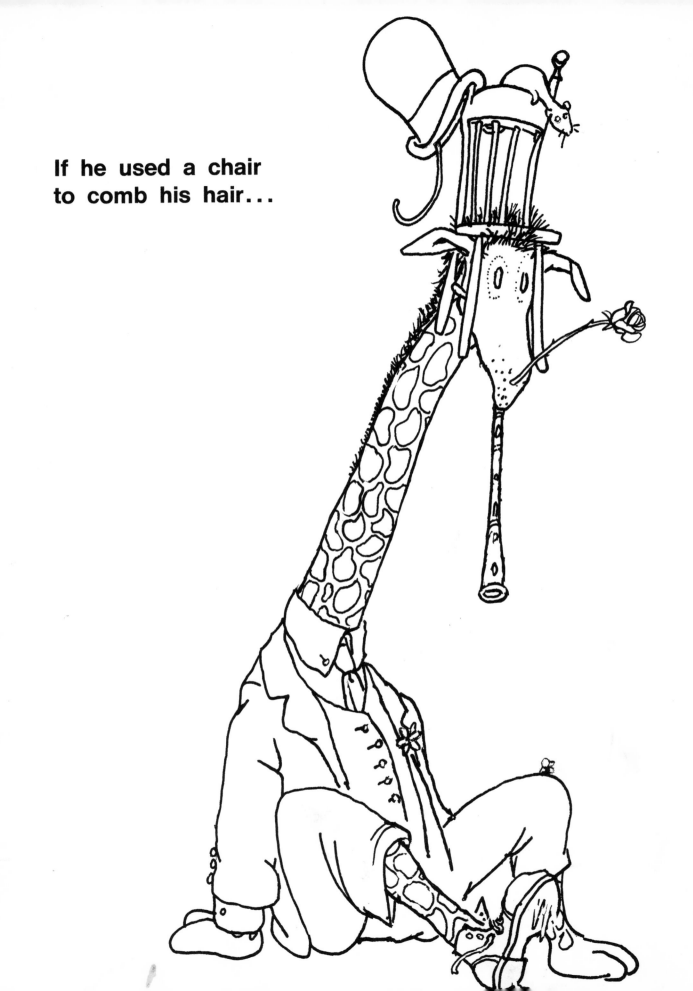

you would have a giraffe and a half
with a rat in his hat
looking cute in a suit
with a rose on his nose
and a bee on his knee
and some glue on his shoe
playing toot on a flute
with a chair in his hair.

If he tripped on a snake
who was eating some cake...

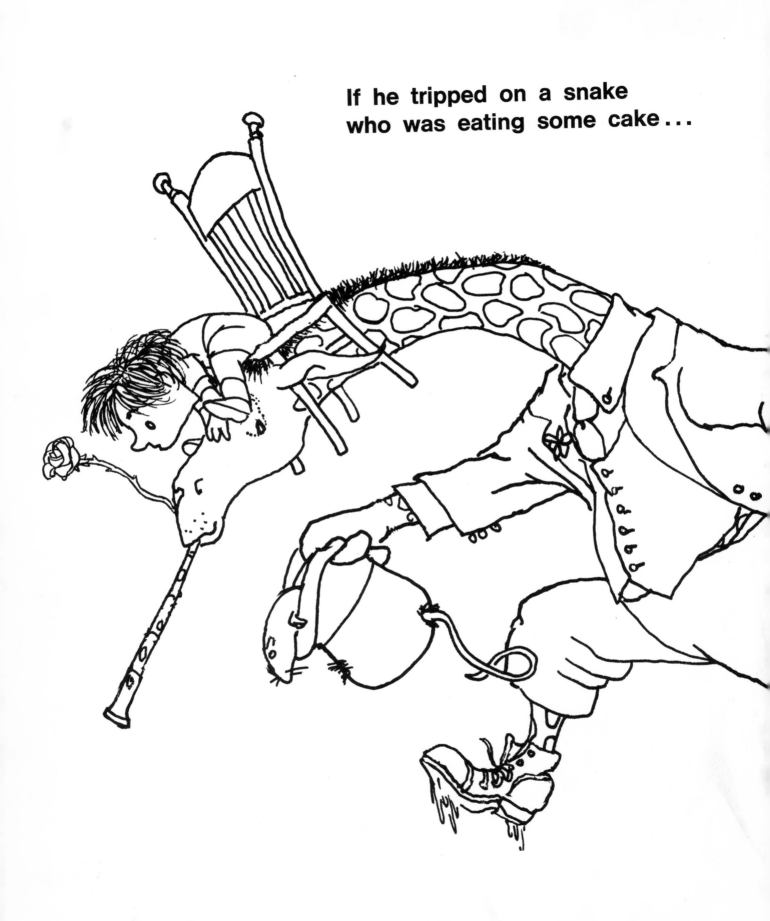

you would have a giraffe and a half
with a rat in his hat
looking cute in a suit
with a rose on his nose
and a bee on his knee
and some glue on his shoe
playing toot on a flute
with a chair in his hair
and a snake eating cake.

If he found an old trunk
and inside was a skunk...

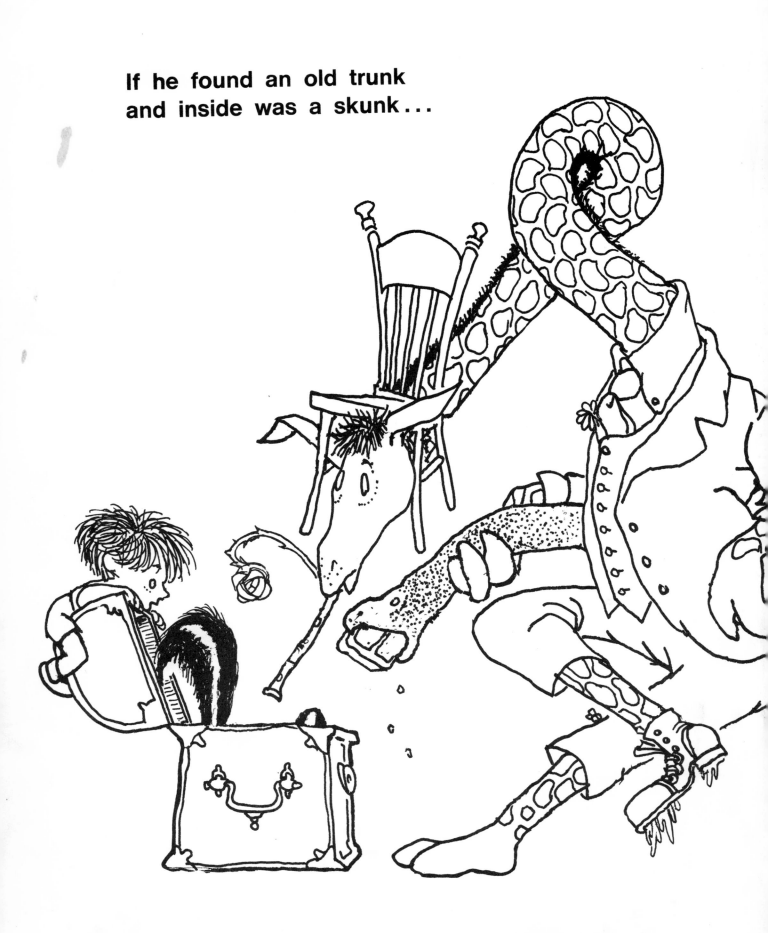

you would have a giraffe and a half
with a rat in his hat
looking cute in a suit
with a rose on his nose
and a bee on his knee
and some glue on his shoe
playing toot on a flute
with a chair in his hair
and a snake eating cake
and a skunk in a trunk.

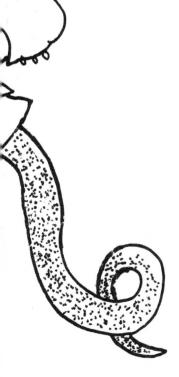

If he met a fat dragon
who sat in a wagon...

you would have a giraffe and a half
with a rat in his hat
looking cute in a suit
with a rose on his nose
and a bee on his knee
and some glue on his shoe
playing toot on a flute
with a chair in his hair
and a snake eating cake
and a skunk in a trunk
and a dragon in a wagon.

**If he jumped on a bike
and rode over a spike...**

you would have a giraffe and a half
with a rat in his hat
looking cute in a suit
with a rose on his nose
and a bee on his knee
and some glue on his shoe
playing toot on a flute
with a chair in his hair
and a snake eating cake
and a skunk in a trunk
and a dragon in a wagon
and a spike in his bike.

If a blubbery whale
got ahold of his tail...

you would have a giraffe and a half
with a rat in his hat
looking cute in a suit
with a rose on his nose
and a bee on his knee
and some glue on his shoe
playing toot on a flute
with a chair in his hair
and a snake eating cake
and a skunk in a trunk
and a dragon in a wagon
and a spike in his bike
and a whale on his tail.

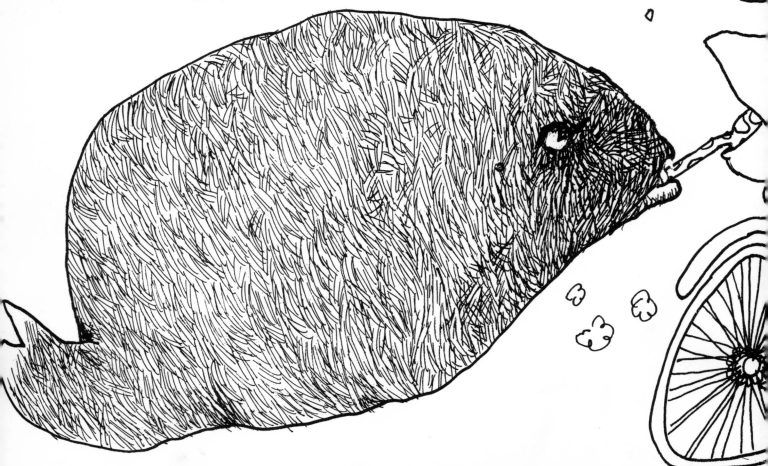

If he fell in a hole
that was dug by a mole...

you would have a giraffe and a half
with a rat in his hat
looking cute in a suit
with a rose on his nose
and a bee on his knee
and some glue on his shoe
playing toot on a flute
with a chair in his hair
and a snake eating cake
and a skunk in a trunk
and a dragon in a wagon
and a spike in his bike
and a whale on his tail
in a hole with a mole.

But . . . if you brought him a pole
to climb out of the hole . . .

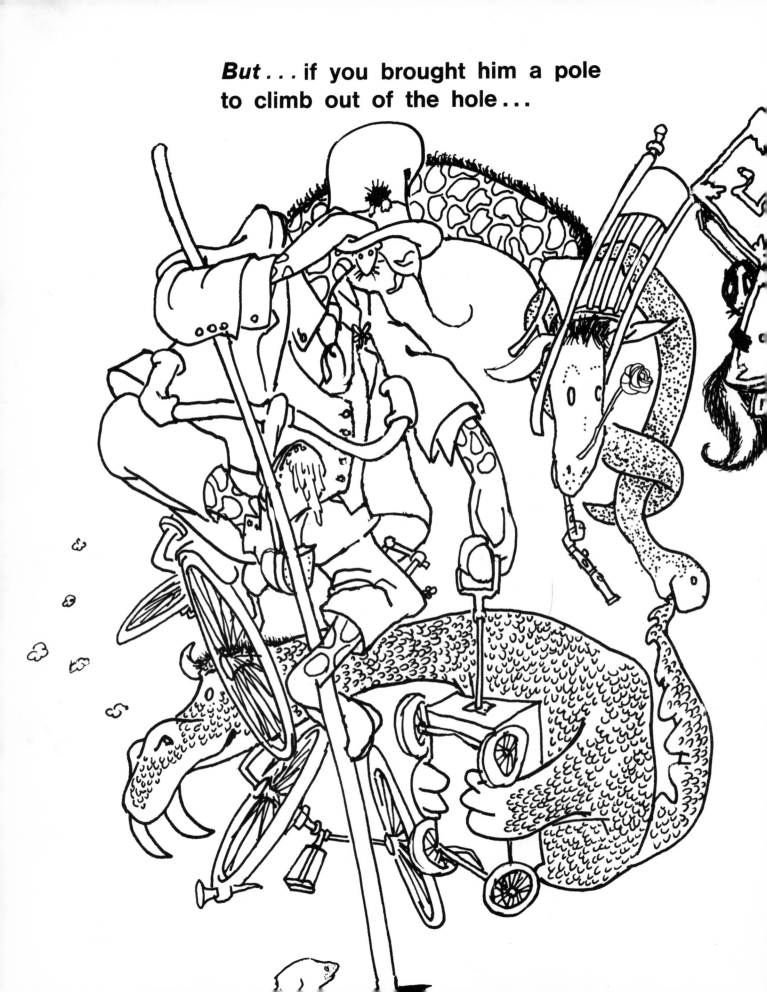

and the whale left his tail
and went off for the mail...

and he gave the spiked bike
to a scout on a hike...

and he left the fat dragon
'cause his wagon was saggin'...

**and he gave his chair
to a tired old bear...**

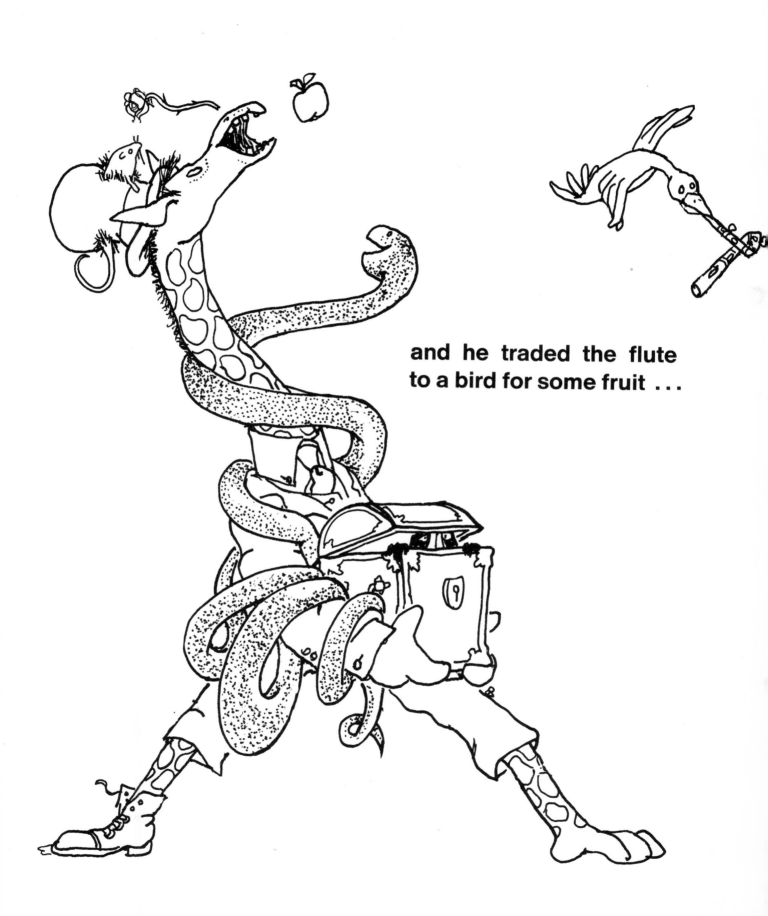

and he traded the flute
to a bird for some fruit . . .

and he told that old snake
to go jump in the lake...

and a man who bought junk
bought the trunk with the skunk...

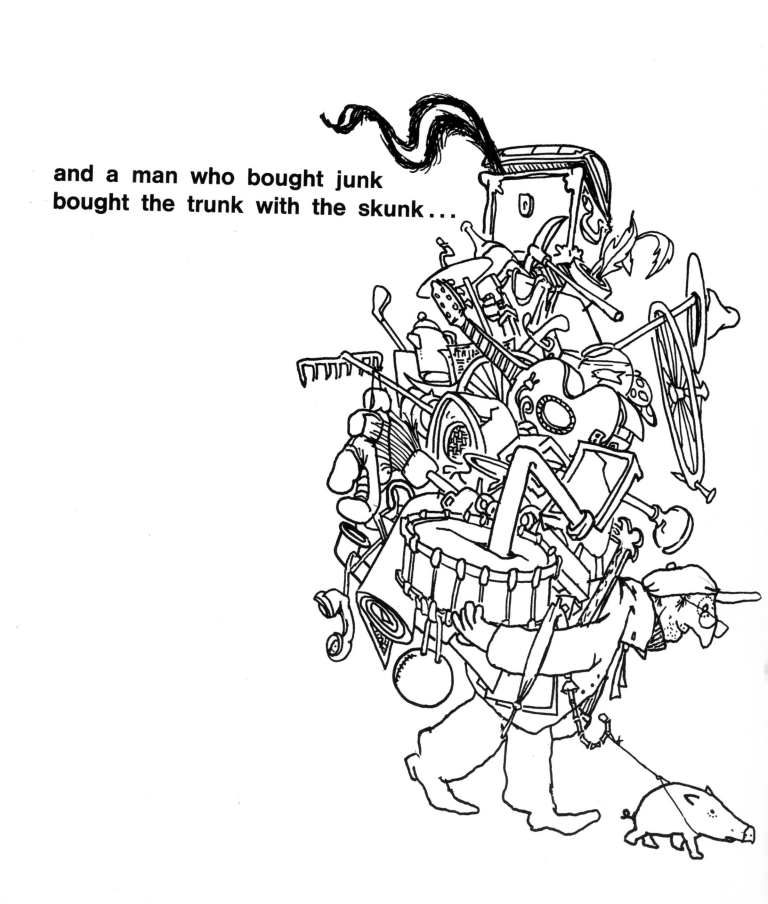

and he gave the rose
to a girl he chose...

while the bee on his knee
flew away with a flea...

and he put the shoe
with the glue
on *you* . . .

**and that silly old rat
ran away with his hat...**

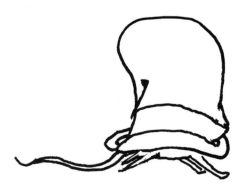

and he put his suit
in the laundry chute...

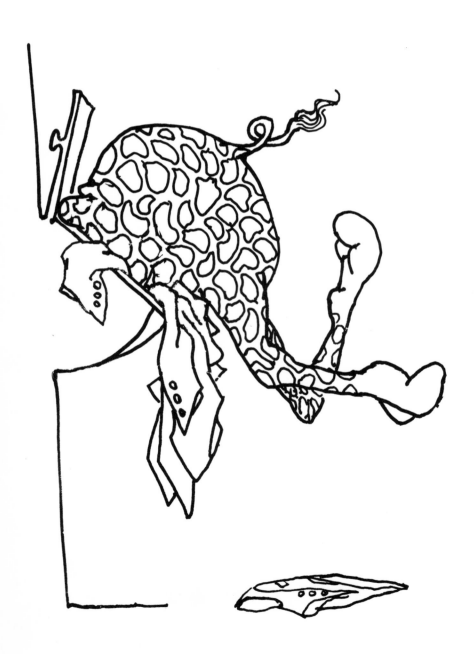

and he shrank another half...

you would have a giraffe!

Silverstein, Shel
A giraffe and a half

DATE DUE			
3-5-87	NOV. 21	5-11-94	
4-8-87	2-2-90	3-22-95	
4-30-87	FEB. 16	3-29-95	
5-7-87	4-26-90	4-5-95	
5-21-87	MAY 11	4-19-95	
11-17-87	3-26-91	4-25-95	
4/19/88	2-25-92	10-11-95	
11-11-88	3-12-92	MAR 12 96	
DEC. 2	12-11-92	APR 2 '98	
1-18-89	11-11-93	APR 16 '98	
3-6-89	4-21-94	MAY 29 96	
10-26-89	5-4-94		

Acc # 3469